See Baby.

See Baby smile for the first time.

See Baby laugh.

Tee
Hee

Laugh, Baby, laugh.

See Daddy jump up and down on one leg and cluck like a chicken to get more laughs.

See Baby crawl.

See Baby crawl **all** over the house.

See Baby **talk** and **talk** and **talk**.

See Baby walk!

Walk, Baby, walk!

See Mommy and Daddy get the camera!

See Baby walk right out the door.

See Baby
make his first
friend.

Look!
Baby has made
LOTS of friends!

See Baby draw a picture.

See Baby draw
LOTS of pictures.

See Baby go potty!

And dress up!

And **swim!**

And have his **first overnight!**

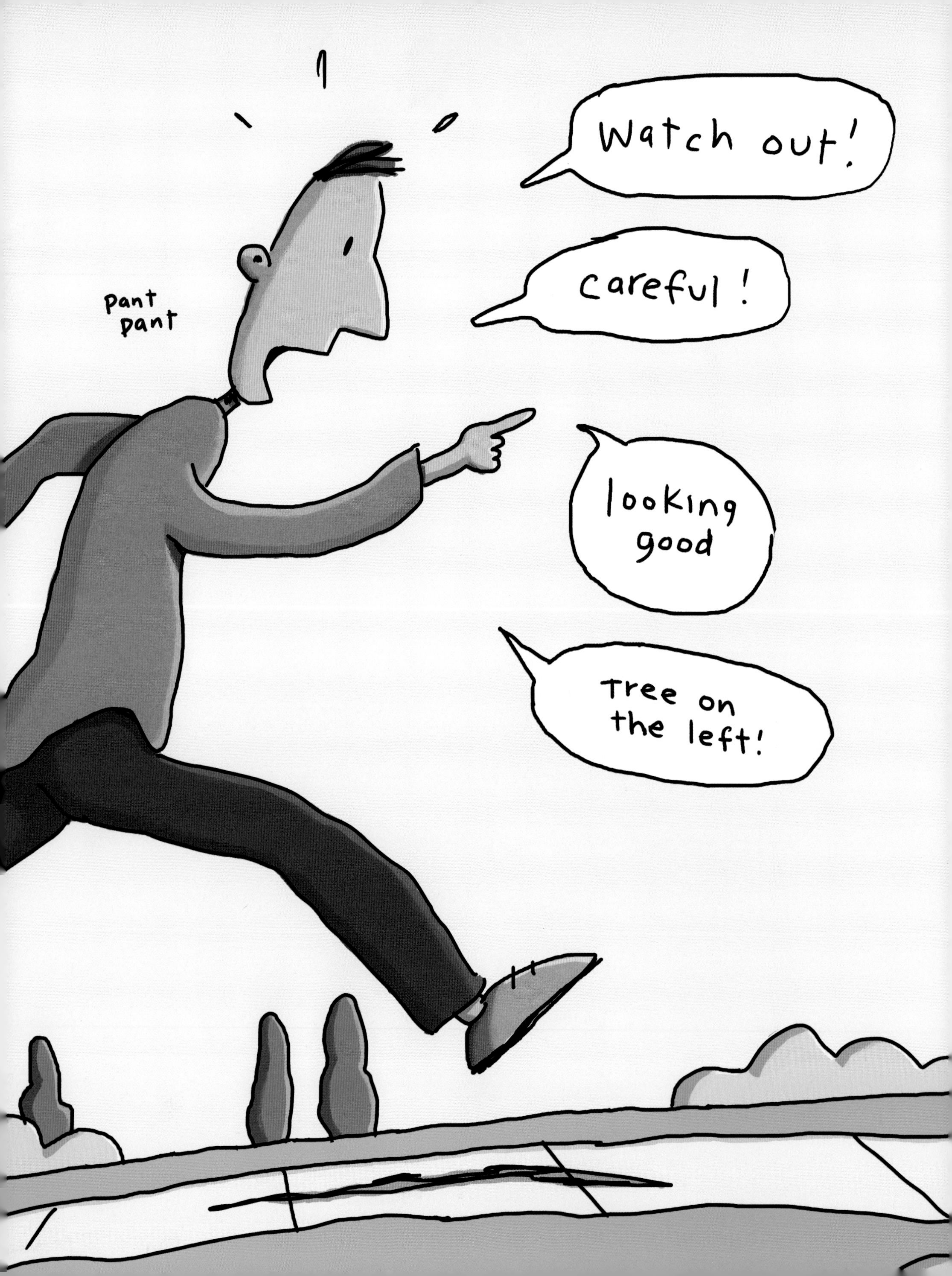
pant
pant
Watch out!
careful!
looking good
Tree on the left!

Baby sure is getting
big and strong.

And fast!

Uh-oh . . .

Where is Baby going **now**?

Look! Baby is getting on a bus!

See Baby go to **school**.

See Baby wave bye-bye.

See Mommy and Daddy cry like two babies.

Baby sure is growing up fast.
Still, he'll always be our baby . . .

The Best Baby Ever!